In The Wild

Penguins

Claire Robinson

Heinemann
LIBRARY

© 1997 Reed Educational & Professional Publishing
Published by Heinemann Interactive Library,
an imprint of Reed Educational & Professional Publishing,
500 Coventry Lane
Crystal Lake, IL 60014

Customer Service 1-888-454-2279

All rights reserved. No part of this publication may be reproduced or transmitted in any form or by any means, electronic, mechanical, including photocopying, recording, taping, or any information storage and retrieval system without permission in writing from the publisher.

Printed in Hong Kong / China
Designed by Celia Floyd
Cover design by Lucy Smith
03 02 01 00 99
10 9 8 7 6 5 4 3 2

The Library of Congress has cataloged the hardcover version of this book as follows:
Library of Congress Cataloging-in-Publication Data

Robinson, Claire, 1955-
   Penguins / Claire Robinson.
     p. cm. -- (In the wild)
   Includes bibliographical references and index.
   Summary: Discusses the lives of penguins, particularly Emperor penguins, describing where they live, what they eat, their mating habits and parental behavior and more.
   ISBN 1-57572-137-6 (lib. bdg.)
   1. Penguins--Juvenile literature. [1. Emperor penguin.
2. Penguins] I. Title. II. Series: Robinson, Claire, 1955-   In the wild.
QL696.S473R635   1997
598. 47--dc21   97-12312
                                                     CIP
                                                     AC

Paperback ISBN 1-57572-468-5

Acknowledgments
The author and publishers are grateful to the following for permission to reproduce copyright photographs:
B. & C. Alexander/H. Reinhard, pp. 7, 11, 12, 12, 13; Ardea London Ltd./Peter Steyn, p. 4 bottom; Bruce Coleman Ltd./Dr. Eckart Pott, p.5 top; Francisco J. Erize, p. 9; Hans Reinhard, p. 10; FLPA/C. Carvalho, p. 4 top, p. 20; M. Horning/Earthviews, p. 21; Oxford Scientific Films/Kjell Sandved, p. 5 bottom, p. 23; Daniel Cox, p. 6; G.I. Kooyman, pp. 8, 22; Doug Allan, pp. 14, 15, 16, 18; Colin Monteath, p. 17; Konrad Wothe, p. 19.

Cover photo: Oxford Scientific Films

Special thanks to Oxford Scientific Films

Every effort has been made to contact copyright holders of any material reproduced in this book. Any omissions will be rectified in subsequent printings if notice is given to the publisher.

Some words are shown in bold, like this. You can find out what they mean by looking in the glossary.

Contents

Penguin Relatives 4
Where Penguins Live 6
Finding Food 8
Coming Ashore 10
Mating.............................12
Eggs 14
Babies..............................16
Growing Up 18
Molting 20
Emperor Penguin Facts......22
Glossary............................*24*
Index *24*
More Books to Read *24*

Penguin Relatives

chinstrap penguins

gentoo penguins

There are 17 different kinds of penguins. They all live in the southern half of the world. Penguins cannot fly, but they are excellent swimmers. They are seabirds.

rockhopper penguins

emperor penguins

Emperor penguins are the largest kind of penguin. Let's see how they live.

Where Penguins Live

Emperor penguins live in the cold seas around **Antarctica**. This is a land covered in ice and snow.

The penguins spend most of the summer in the water. They come ashore to **breed** and **molt**.

Finding Food

The penguins are very fast and **agile** swimmers. When they want food, they dive deep in search of fish and **squid**.

There is danger in the sea. This leopard seal is a fierce hunter that eats penguins, but it can only catch them in the water!

Coming Ashore

It is fall and the penguins come ashore to breed. They swim fast under water toward the land. Then they shoot upward and land on the ice.

Penguins cannot walk fast. Sometimes they flop onto their tummies and push themselves along with their feet. This is called **tobogganing**. It is fun, and quick!

Mating

The emperors are on their long journey across the ice. They travel to the place where they lay their eggs each year.

Emperor penguins have the same partner for life. Now they find their partners after five months apart. They do a dance called a **mating display**.

Eggs

After three weeks, the female lays one large egg. Then she **treks** back to sea to find food. The male guards the egg. He keeps it warm on his feet under a flap of skin.

It is freezing cold. The males all **huddle** together. They cannot feed because they are looking after the eggs, so they live off the fat in their bodies.

Babies

Two months later, the eggs hatch. The mothers return from the sea to care for the chicks. At last the hungry fathers are free to go off in search of food.

Emperor chicks are covered in **downy**, gray feathers. After a few weeks, they are too big to sit on their mother's feet.

Growing Up

Both parents travel back and forth across the ice, collecting food from the sea. This father feeds his growing chick with half-eaten fish.

The chicks grow up in large groups watched over by adult penguins. There are hundreds of them in the **rookery**.

Molting

As summer draws near, the young penguins **molt**. Shiny new feathers push out the old ones. Now the birds are waterproof and ready to swim.

The ice over the sea has melted. The young penguins dive in for the first time. Next year, if they live, they will return here to molt.

Emperor Penguin Facts

- Emperor penguins are the largest kind of penguin. They are over three feet tall.

- Their flipper-like wings are very powerful. They can dive deeper than most seabirds.

- Emperors can live for 20 years. They have their first chicks when they are about five years old.

- Males and females look the same, but they make different sounds.

Glossary

agile Quick and graceful.
Antarctica Continent of mountains and ice at the southern tip of the world.
breed Have babies.
downy Soft and fluffy.
huddle Keep very close together.
mating Two animals making a baby together.
mating display Kind of dance that males and females do before mating.
molt Lose old feathers and grow new ones.
rookery Large group of penguins.
squid Sea animal with eight trailing arms.
tobogganing Sliding across the snow.
trek Make a difficult journey.

Index

chicks   17, 18, 19, 21, 23
eggs   12, 14, 15, 16
feathers   17, 20
feeding   8, 15, 16, 18
females   14, 16, 17, 23
finding food   8, 16, 18
keeping warm   14, 15
males   14, 15, 16, 18, 23
molting   7, 20, 21
swimming   4, 7, 8, 10, 20, 22
traveling   10, 11, 12, 14, 18

More Books To Read

Cousteau Society Staff. *Penguins*. New York: Simon & Schuster Children's, 1992.
Fontanel, Beatrice and Tracqui, Valerie. *The Penguin: Animal Close-Ups*. Watertown, Mass.: Charlesbridge, 1992.
Ling, Mary. *Penguin*. New York: Dorling Kindersley, 1993.